Dear Parent:
Your child's love of reading starts here!

Every child learns to read in a different way and at his or her own
speed. Some go back and forth between reading levels and read
favorite books again and again. Others read through each level in
order. You can _____ become more
confident by en _____ bilities. From
books your ch _____ r she reads
alone, there ar _____ iding:

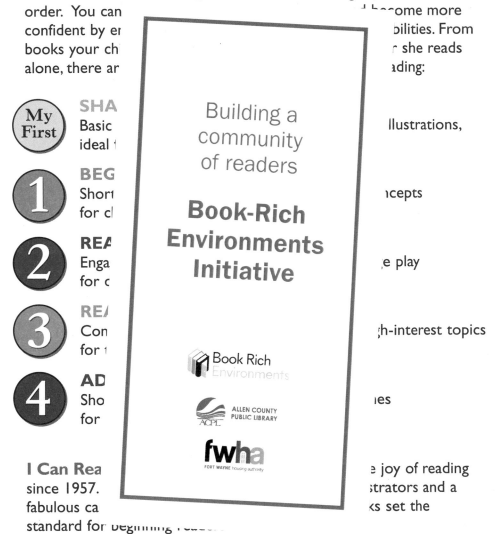

My First — SHA
Basic _____ llustrations,
ideal f

1 — BEG
Short _____ icepts
for cl

2 — REA
Enga _____ e play
for c

3 — REA
Con _____ h-interest topics
for

4 — AD
Sho _____ ies
for

I Can Rea _____ e joy of reading
since 1957. _____ strators and a
fabulous ca _____ ks set the
standard for beginning _____

A lifetime of discovery begins with the magical words **"I Can Read!"**

Visit www.icanread.com for information
on enriching your child's reading experience.

ISBN 978-0-545-86457-2

18 17   18 19 20/0

Printed in the U.S.A.   40

First Scholastic printing, September 2015

I Can Read!™ SHARED My First READING

Pete the Cat
TOO COOL FOR SCHOOL

by Kimberly and James Dean

SCHOLASTIC INC.

Pete wants to look cool.

He asks everyone,

"What should I wear?"

"Wear your yellow shirt,"
his mom says.
"It is my favorite."

So Pete does.

"Wear your red shirt,"
Pete's friend Marty says.
"It is my favorite."

So Pete does.

"Wear your blue shirt,"
Pete's brother Bob says.
"It is my favorite."

So Pete does.

"Wear your long pants,"
Pete's teacher says.
"They are my favorite."

2+2=4

So Pete does.

"Wear the shorts with the fish,"
Pete's friend Callie says.
"They are my favorite."

So Pete does.

"Wear the polka-dot socks,"
the bus driver says.
"They are my favorite."

So Pete does.

"Wear the cowboy boots,"
Grumpy Toad says.
"They are my favorite."

So Pete does.

"Wear the tie with the stripes,"
Emma says.

"It is my favorite."

So Pete does.

"Wear your baseball hat,"
his coach says.
"It is my favorite."

So Pete does.

Pete puts on all the clothes.

Does he look cool?

No.

Pete looks silly.

He also feels very hot!

Pete goes home.

He changes his clothes.

Pete puts on HIS favorite shirt.

Pete puts on HIS favorite pants.

Pete puts on HIS favorite socks.

Pete puts on HIS favorite shoes.

Pete puts on his sunglasses.

Pete says, "Now I am COOL."

If you want to be cool,
just be you!